RUNAWAY
The Story of a Slave

Dee Phillips

READZONE

First published in this edition 2013

ReadZone Books Limited
50 Godfrey Avenue
Twickenham
TW2 7PF
UK

British Library Cataloguing in Publication Data (CIP) is available for this title.

ISBN 978-1-78322-008-3

Printed in China

Developed and Created by Ruby Tuesday Books Ltd
Project Director – Ruth Owen
Designer – Elaine Wilkinson

Images are in the public domain or courtesy of Shutterstock.

Acknowledgements
With thanks to Lorraine Petersen, Chief Executive of NASEN, for her help in the development and creation of these books

Visit our website: www.readzonebooks.com

I was born a slave.

The master owned me.

He owned my mother and father.

RUNAWAY

The Story of a Slave

In the year 1850 many people in America had slaves.

The slaves were people from Africa.
They were forced to go to America.
They were treated like prisoners.

The slaves were forced to work hard.
Many slaves were whipped.
Some slaves were killed.

Some tried
to escape...

The moon is bright.
I run as fast as I can.
Stones cut my feet to pieces.
But I don't stop.
I will never go back.

I hear a howl.
My heart beats fast.
It's the master and his dogs!

The dogs will tear me to pieces.

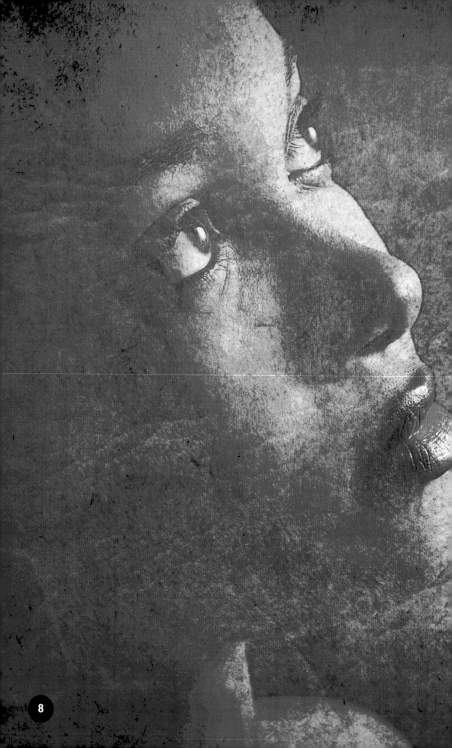

I stop. I listen.
There are no dogs.
Just wolves howling at the bright moon.
I run as fast as I can.
I will never go back.

I was born a slave.
The master owned me.
He owned my mother and father.

I will never forget the day they
took my father.
The master wanted money.
He wanted to sell us.
He took us to the town.
I held my mother's hand tight.

Men and women looked at us.

I heard a voice shout, "Sold."
My father shouted, "No! No!"
My mother screamed, "Take us, too!"
A man led my father away.
But he didn't want to buy us.

We never saw
my father again.

13

I run as fast as I can.
My heart beats fast.
My body feels heavy and tired.

But I don't stop.

I will never go back.

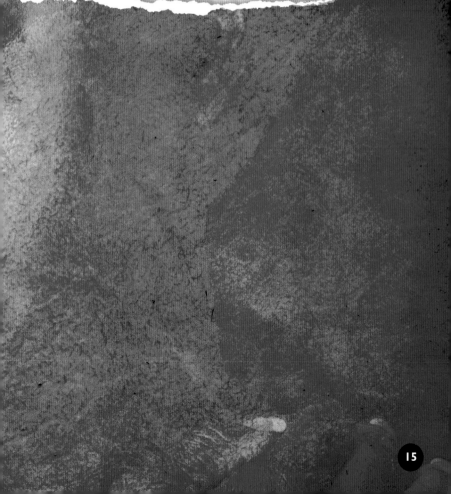

Soon the sun will rise.

Then I will rest.

I will hide until it is night.

Then I will run again.

I have many miles to go.

I was born a slave.
But inside I was free.

I grew taller and stronger.
The master made me work.
I picked cotton in the fields.
The cotton cut my hands to pieces.

The years passed.
My mother died.
I wanted to run away.

An old slave told a story.
A story about a place many miles away.
A place where there were no slaves.
I asked the slave about this place.

I will never forget that day.

The master took me into the barn.
He pulled the dress from my back.
"I hear you want to run
away, Mary," he hissed.

I felt his whip on my back.
It slashed at my skin again and again.
My body was cut to pieces.
I wanted to die.

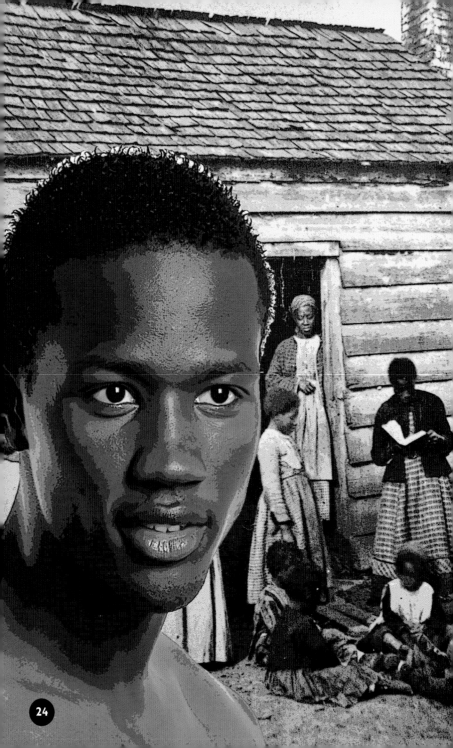

Then Tomas came to the farm.
Tomas was tall and strong.
We picked cotton together.
We fell in love.

Tomas asked me to be his wife.
We lived in a cabin on the farm.

I watch the sun rise.
Now I can rest.
My body feels heavy and tired.

Tonight I will run again.

Run to the place where
there are no slaves.

One day I could not work.
My body was too tired.

The master came to our cabin.
He pulled me from the bed.
"You lazy, dirty slave," he hissed.

I felt his whip slash at my
skin again and again.

That night Tomas came back from the fields.
I saw the anger in his eyes.

Tomas was born a slave.
But inside he was free.
Tomas was not afraid of the master.

Tomas ran from our cabin.
He ran to the master's house.

The other slaves brought Tomas
back to the cabin.
His legs were broken.
His face was cut to pieces.
His eyes were blind.
He died in my arms.

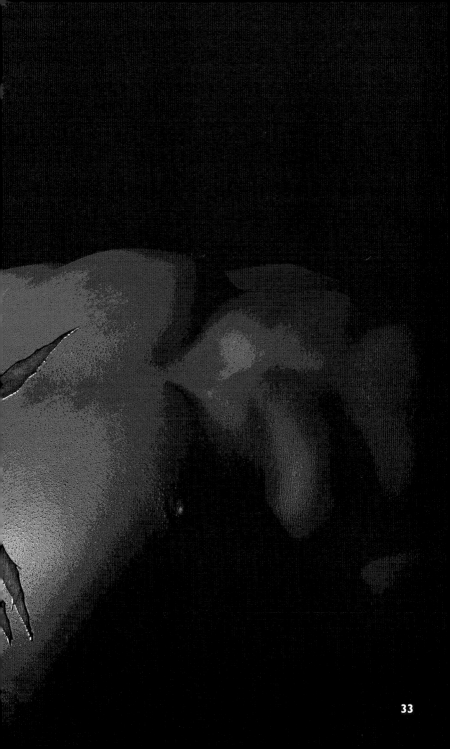

I watch the moon rise.
My body feels heavy and tired.
I feel a pain inside me.
But I must keep going.

After Tomas died, I made my plan.
I talked to the other slaves.
They told me about a
secret group of people.

This secret group helps runaway slaves.
They told me how to find these people.

I walk all night.
Then I see the house.
A candle burns in the window.
It is a secret sign.
The people in this house help
runaway slaves.

A woman opens the door.
The pain inside me grows stronger.
"Am I free?" I ask her.
The woman nods.

*"Yes child.
You are free now."*

I go into the house.

The pain grows. . .

stronger. . .

and stronger.

Then I hear my baby cry.

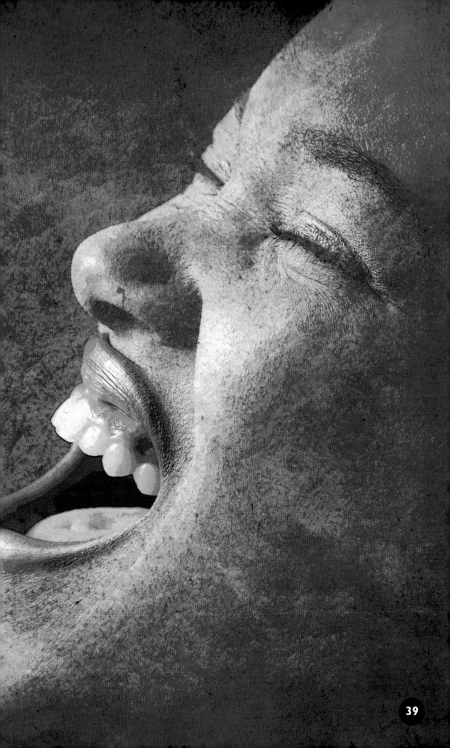

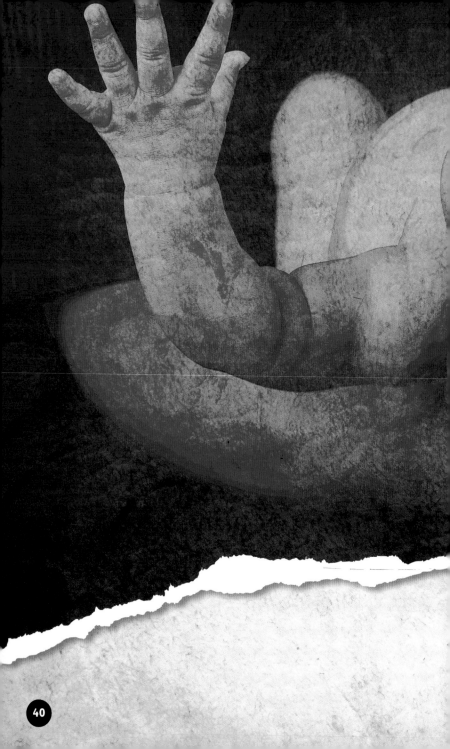

I was born a slave.
But now I am free.
I hold my tiny son.

I say, "You are free, little Tomas."

Runaway:
Behind the Story

In the 1600s and 1700s, slave traders from Europe and America kidnapped people from their villages in Africa. The captives were then taken to America on slave ships.

As slaves, people were forced to do work such as picking tobacco, cotton and other crops.

In the 1800s, some Americans helped slaves escape to Canada or parts of America where slavery was illegal. These people formed the Underground Railroad.

The Underground Railroad was a network of secret escape routes, with stops along the way. These stops were usually at the homes of people who hid runaway slaves. They then guided the runaways to the next stop, usually at night.

Slavery lasted in many parts of the United States until 1865. At that time, the US government made it illegal to own slaves anywhere in the country. By 1865, four million African Americans were living as slaves.

The Underground Railroad helped up to 100,000 runaway slaves escape to freedom.

This painting shows a family helping a group of runaway slaves.

Runaway – *What's next?*

RUNNING
ON YOUR OWN

Imagine you are Mary running away from the master. Write down all the things you feel as you make your escape. For example:

I feel afraid. I want to be free.
I don't want to die.

Organise your feelings into a poem. Try repeating one line throughout the poem.

> I feel afraid.
> I want to be free.
> I don't want to die.
> I want to be free.
> I miss Tomas.
> I want to be free.

INSIDE I WAS FREE
ON YOUR OWN / WITH A PARTNER / IN A GROUP

In the story Mary says, "I was born a slave. But inside I was free."

- What do you think Mary means?

- In what ways could a person who was a slave feel or be free?

Mary and Tomas are characters in a story. What happened to them, however, is based on the real life stories of millions of people who were forced to live as slaves. Discuss the story and what you've learned about slavery with your group.

- How would it feel to be owned by another person?

- What was it like to be sold and perhaps separated from your family forever?

- What did you feel when the master whipped Mary? And when Tomas was killed?

FROM SLAVERY TO FREEDOM
ON YOUR OWN / WITH A PARTNER / IN A GROUP

Make a collage that shows Mary's life before and after she runs away.

Use images, colours and words to tell her story.

Titles in the
Yesterday's Voices
series

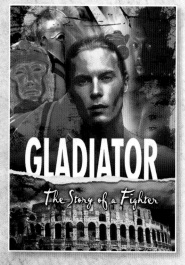

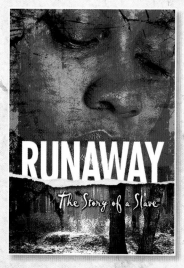

I waited deep below the arena. Then it was my turn to fight. Kill or be killed!

I cannot live as a slave any longer. Tonight, I will escape and never go back.

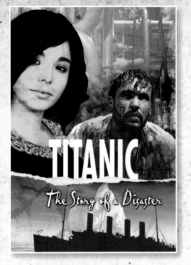

TITANIC
The Story of a Disaster

The ship is sinking into the icy sea. I don't want to die. Someone help us!

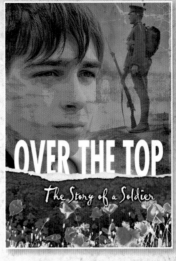

OVER THE TOP
The Story of a Soldier

I'm waiting in the trench. I am so afraid. Tomorrow, we go over the top.

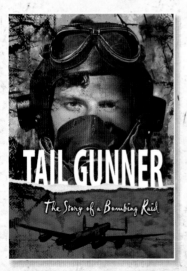

TAIL GUNNER
The Story of a Bombing Raid

Another night. Another bombing raid. Will this night be the one when we don't make it back?

HOLOCAUST
The Story of a Survivor

They took my clothes and shaved my head. I was no longer a human.